Our community has a new, rather unique little squirrel. Here's his story.

Earl the Squirrel

Dedicated to Pam Gilbert
who wouldn't take "No" for an answer.

Published by Make Me a Story Press (MMASP)
P. O. Box 151, Watseka, IL 60970

MMASP Attn: Permissions, 1737 N 2580 E Rd., Sheldon, IL 60966

Library of Congress Number: 2005925558

ISBN   9781878847003

Printed in China First Edition, July 2005

Right from the beginning
Earl was different
than other squirrels.

He had one
enormous
front tooth.

As Earl grew,

his tooth grew too.

That tooth made it
hard to whistle.

And, as you might expect,

he had to use twice as much tooth paste.

All the other squirrels in the neighborhood

knew who he was on Halloween.

Although there was a solution
to that problem.

There were no **big** problems, until...

PSS #7

...Earl's first day of school.

Everything went wrong.

It was all the tooth's fault.

Earl ran home crying.
He cried so hard, he could hardly see.

Then to make matters worse,

Earl tripped over his own tooth...

...and he fell.

Without knowing
quite how,

Earl found himself
having fun.

He was using his big tooth
to snag a limb here,

and a branch there.

All at once, and for the first time,

he really liked that tooth.

His tooth had a wonderful new use.

More importantly,
Earl discovered that
the more he liked his
tooth,

the more he liked
himself, and the
more he smiled.

That big smile helped Earl make new friends.

And, everyone sang;
"You were born
a year ago,
a year ago
today,

we baked a cake
to celebrate,

so blow
the candle
out."

Then Earl closed
his eyes

and made
a wish.

What do you suppose

Earl wished for?

This storybook asks one question at the end, in which the child's answer tends to be better than to adult's!

There are no wrong or right answers, of course, but...

Give it a try, and see if you don't agree.

Be patient, children probably won't even venture a guess until after several readings. Expect an "I don't know." at first.

THE COUNTRY SQUIRREL

Occasionally prompt for an answer after a reading. A response will come in time.

Be careful not to divulge your answer, hopefully it's written down somewhere.

Current Releases

Book 1 — Earl the Squirrel
Book 3 — Earl Joins the Circus

Scheduled (2006) Releases

Making Friends

Smile School

Ground Squirrel School

That Smell

On the Trail

Sign in here _____